THE PHANTOM STRIKER

Jonny Zucker

D1585701

Illustrated by Victor Tavares

Titles in First Flight

Badger Publishing Limited
15 Wedgwood Gate, Pin Green Industrial Estate,
Stevenage, Hertfordshire SG1 4SU
Telephone: 01438 356907. Fax: 01438 747015
www.badger-publishing.co.uk
enquiries@badger-publishing.co.uk

The Phantom Striker ISBN 1 84424 817 8

Text © Jonny Zucker 2006
Complete work © Badger Publishing Limited 2006

Series Editor: Jonny Zucker
Publisher: David Jamieson
Commissioning Editor: Carrie Lewis
Editor: Paul Martin
Design: Fiona Grant
Illustration: Victor Tavares

THE PHANTOM STRIKER

Jonny Zucker

Contents

The Red Door

Tom and Dan were in Wood End School football team. Mr Lot was the team coach.

The team were bad.
They were very, very bad.

They had played ten games.
They had lost ten games.
Mr Lot wanted them to win just one game.

Tom and Dan were sitting in the playground.

"I'm fed up with the football team," said Tom.

"I'm fed up too," said Dan. "We're rubbish."

"What we need is a great new player," said Dan.

"But all our best players are in the team," said Tom.

"Maybe I can help," a voice said.

"Who was that?" asked Tom.

Tom and Dan looked around. No one was there.

The voice had come from behind a wall. There was a strange red door in the wall.

They had never seen the red door before.

"What shall we do?" asked Dan.

Tom walked over to it.
"Let's open it," he said.

Tom opened the red door and
the boys walked through it.
It led to a very misty field.

"Where are we?" asked Tom.

"I don't know," replied Dan.

Suddenly a strange, strong-looking
boy appeared.

He was wearing a football kit.
He was carrying a football under
his arm.

But there was something else –
Tom and Dan could see straight
through him!

Dan started to scream.

"Don't be afraid," said the boy.
"My name is Hamish."

"We can see through you,"
said Tom.

"That's because I'm a ghost," said Hamish.

"A real ghost?" asked Dan.

Hamish nodded. "I'm a football ghost. I can only come out when someone wants me to help them."

"Like when I said our team
needed a new player?" said Tom.

"That's right," nodded Hamish.
"No one else but you two can see
me. When do you need me?"

Tom and Dan looked at each
other.

"We've got a match today," said Dan.

"Great!" grinned Hamish.

"What do we need to do?" asked Tom.

"Don't do anything," smiled Hamish. "Just watch me!"

The match was after school.

"Come on everyone," said Mr Lot.
"Try and win just one game!"

Early on in the game, Dan had
a shot.

It was going wide, but Hamish
grabbed the ball and flung it into
the back of the net!

"Great goal Dan!" shouted
Mr Lot.

Ten minutes later, Tom headed
the ball in the air. It was about to
fall back on the ground when
Hamish jumped up and held it.

He ran down the pitch and threw
it into the goal.

Mr Lot and the crowd went wild.
No one had ever seen a header
like that!

At the end of the game it was 2-0
to Wood End School. The team
had won their first ever match!

Mr Lot was very, very happy.

Tom and Dan thanked Hamish.

"You're the best!" grinned Dan.

Hamish grinned back.

The next match was 0-0 until nearly half time.

A player suddenly shot the ball towards the Wood End goal. The Wood End goalkeeper dived but missed it. The ball was going in.

Suddenly Hamish ran up and kicked the ball away.

Mr Lot couldn't believe it. It was the best save ever.

Wood End won their next three matches. Hamish ran all over the place, scoring goals and making great saves.

Everyone in the area heard about
the Wood End team suddenly
doing well.

Billy Blunt at Green Street school
heard about the matches.
Billy was big and very tough.

"Wood End are rubbish!" he said.
"They must be cheating."

The next game was the last one
of the season.

It was Wood End v Green Street.

"I'll show them," said Billy Blunt.

The Last Match

Early on in the match, Billy took a shot. It sped to the Wood End goal.

Hamish got to the ball and pushed it over the bar.

"Hey!" shouted Billy. "That was going in! Wood End are cheats!"

In the second half, Dan took
a corner. The ball was going out.
Then Hamish got it and ran with it
into the goal.

"What's going on?" yelled
Billy Blunt.

At the end of the game, it was
1-0 to Wood End.

Billy Blunt was
really mad.

Dan and Tom went over to say thanks to Hamish. But Billy Blunt followed them.

"You were great!" Dan said to Hamish.

"Brilliant!" said Tom.

"Over here!" screamed Billy.
"These two are talking to
someone. I knew they were
cheating!"

Everyone ran over. Billy was
standing next to Tom and Dan.
There was no one else there.

Muddy Ears

"Who were they talking to?"
asked Mr Lot.

At that moment, Hamish grabbed
Billy Blunt and spun him round.
Billy fell backwards into a big
muddy puddle.

"They were talking to someone!" Billy shouted, his face covered in mud.

"I think you are hearing things," said Mr Lot. "There must be too much mud between your ears."

Everyone laughed at Billy.

Later on, Tom and Dan walked
with Hamish to the playground.

"The football matches are all
over now," said Tom.

"It's been great," replied Hamish.

"Come and call for me next year, when the football games start again."

"We will," said Dan.

Hamish waved and walked off through the red door.

Basketball Blues

Two weeks later, Tom and Dan went to the playground after school and called for Hamish.

"Hi boys," grinned Hamish, coming through the red door. "I didn't think the football matches had started yet."

"They haven't," said Dan.

"Then why do you both look so unhappy?" asked Hamish.

"Mr Lot wants to start a basketball team," said Tom.

"So?" asked Hamish.

"We're all very bad at basketball," replied Dan. "And we know you only play football. So we're really stuck."

Hamish started laughing.

"What's so funny?" asked Tom.

"You haven't met my brother, have you?" grinned Hamish.

The boys shook their heads.

"JACK!" shouted Hamish.

Suddenly, out of the mist, ran a very tall, see-through boy.

"Does someone need me?" he asked with a grin.

Tom and Dan smiled.

Jack was wearing a green vest top and was spinning a basketball on his finger.